Grandma Bendy

by Izy Penguin

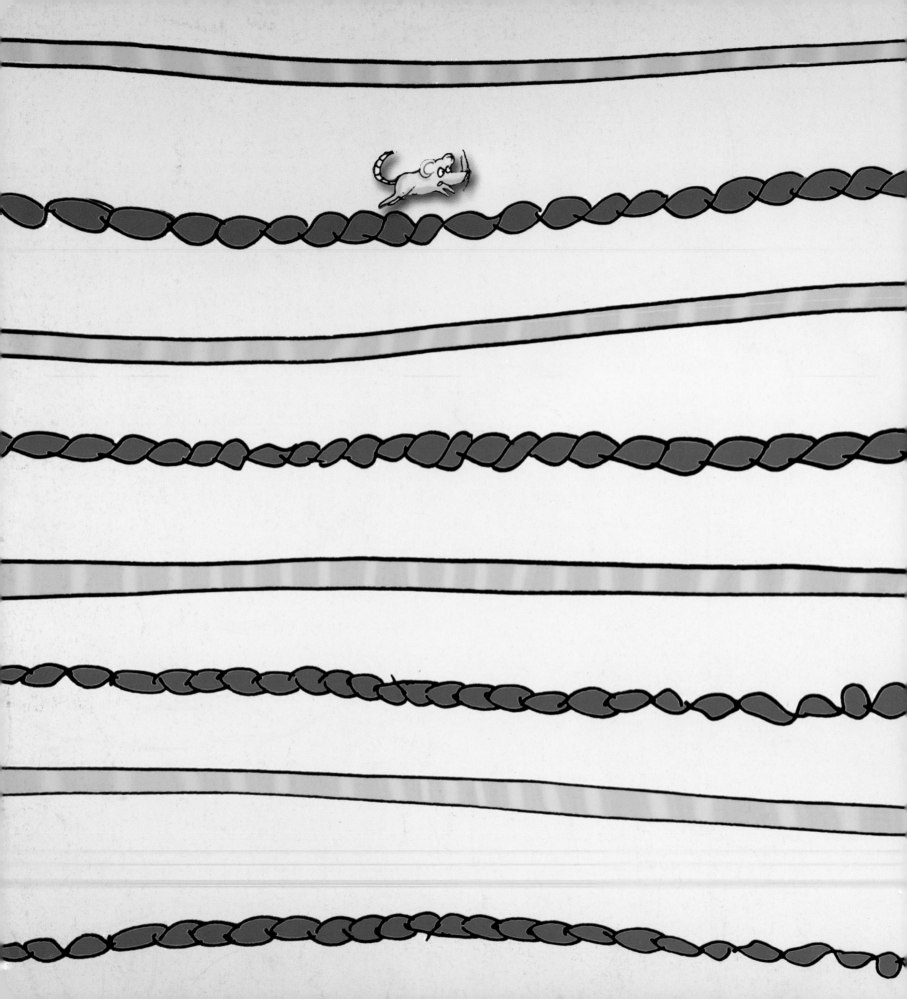

Our Grandma isn't like
any other Grandma.

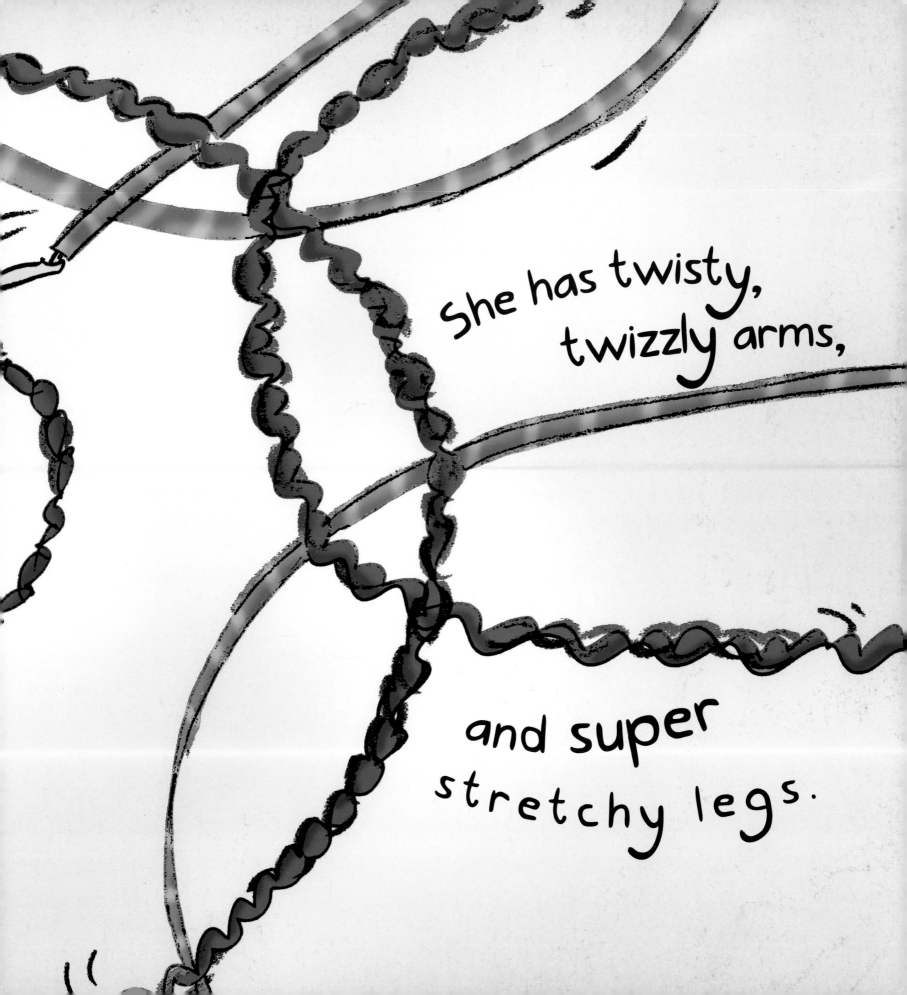

She has twisty, twizzly arms,

and super stretchy legs.

This makes her very good at hide and seek!

However, in the olden days, Grandma Bendy told us she was very, very bad and lived a life of crime...

Bad Bendy

FLAKES OF CORN-O

Grandma Bendy used to be a brilliant burglar.
She could bend and twizzle her way in and out
of houses, squeezing through the tiniest of spaces.

Then one day...

She came home to find that she had been **burgled!**

All of her favourite things had been stolen. This made her feel sad and very ashamed.

What will Bendy wear?

The rotters have nicked the goldfish!

So ashamed of herself that Grandma Bendy went straight to the police. She told them about the bad things she'd done. But just as Grandma Bendy was feeling better, the police...

But then one day, she spotted her neighbour was **locked** out of her house and if there was one thing that Grandma Bendy knew, it was how to get into **houses**.

Without thinking, her legs stretched and her arms **twizzled their** way in through the letterbox, all the way up to the lock and opened her neighbour's door.

Bending over backwards to help people made Grandma Bendy feel good.

This gave her a **BIG** idea!

She **decided** that from now on, she would use her bendiness to **help people!**

Now everyone **loves** Grandma Bendy and **her** brilliantly bendy ways.

That is why Grandma Bendy is the **best Grandma** around!

The End.

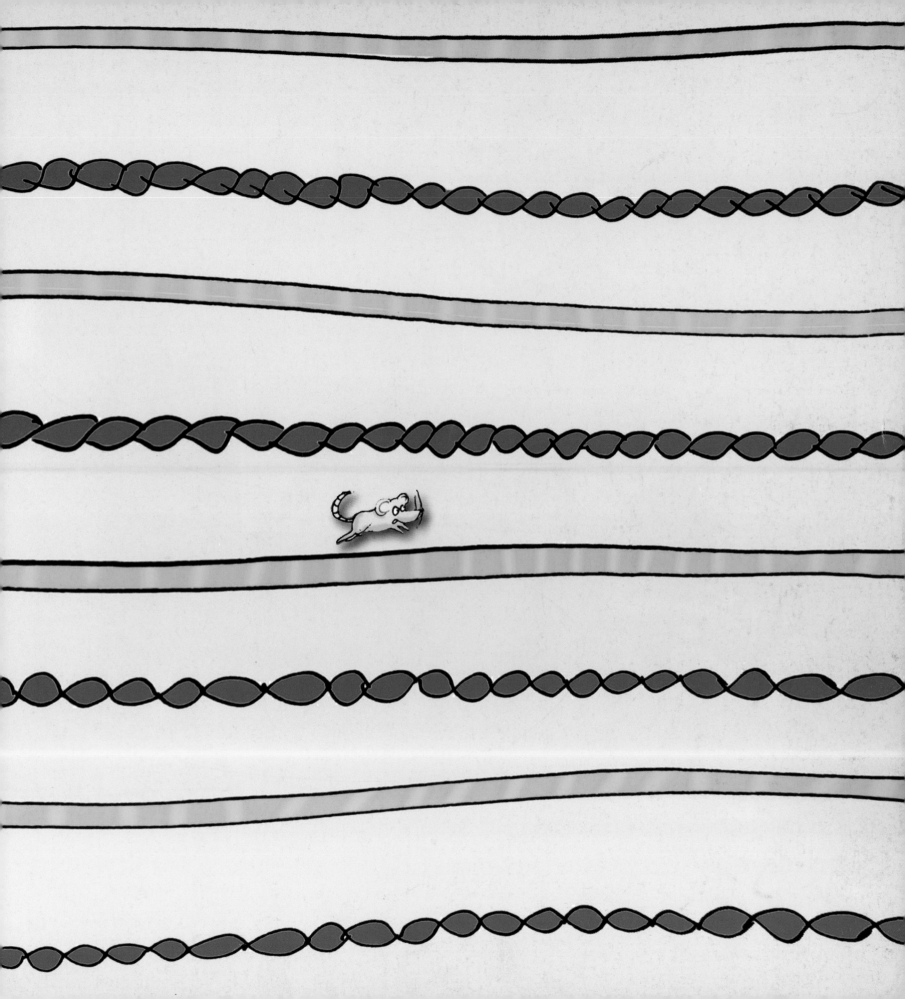

Grandma Bendy
is an original concept by
© Izy Penguin
Author : Izy Penguin

Illustrated by Izy Penguin

A CIP catalogue record for this book
is available from the British Library.

ISBN 978-1-84886-077-3

**PUBLISHED BY MAVERICK ARTS
PUBLISHING LTD**
©Maverick Arts Publishing Limited (2012)
2nd edition 2014

Studio 3A, City Business Centre,
6 Brighton Road,
Horsham,
West Sussex, RH13 5BB
+44(0) 1403 256941

Maverick
arts publishing

www.maverickbooks.co.uk

**THIS EDITION PUBLISHED
2014 FOR INDEX BOOKS**